Pink Loon

A. E. Howard

authorHOUSE®

AuthorHouse™
1663 Liberty Drive
Bloomington, IN 47403
www.authorhouse.com

This is a work of fiction. All of the characters, names, incidents, organizations, and dialogue in this work are either the products of the author's imagination or are used fictitiously.

Published by AuthorHouse   01/10/2019

ISBN: 978-1-5462-7464-3 (sc)
ISBN: 978-1-5462-7466-7 (hc)
ISBN: 978-1-5462-7465-0 (e)

Library of Congress Control Number: 2019900193

Print information available on the last page.

This book is printed on acid-free paper.

Because of the dynamic nature of the Internet, any web addresses or links contained in this book may have changed since publication and may no longer be valid. The views expressed in this work are solely those of the author and do not necessarily reflect the views of the publisher, and the publisher hereby disclaims any responsibility for them.

CONTENTS

For:
Mama, Pop
and
Dr. Wil Cheshier

1

I think my cat is sick of me. She doesn't even sit in the same room as I.

The first time I've been out of my apartment in almost 4 days. Have to return a form to my landlord. Finally, an excuse. The mailbox is on the corner. I get the same form every year: do you have kids under 6 years old, under 11 years old, and do you have peeling lead paint and window guards? I have bars on the windows, they were there when I moved in. Maybe some peeling paint, but I'm not interested in eating any of it, and I don't think my cat is either.

Whenever I look out my window at night, I see those bars. Sometimes I grab them. Prison bars. Gotta make a break. Gotta find life on the outside.

January is a dark time of year for me. It's my least favorite month. Cold, silent, the mounds of charcoal snow on the street corners and in front of the subway entrances are the worst. The harshness of metal on metal as I release the mailbox handle. The squeal of the braking F train arriving draws me down the stairs. Navigating the subway steps places my life in the hands of the gods of a frictionless universe.

A homeless guy on the downtown F train has two Food Emporium bags on his feet held on by two rubber bands over his shoes. Crazy, but his feet are probably drier than mine. Mine are wet and freezing. I climb up the stairs at the Second Avenue stop. Howling wind.

Hoping to find life, I see none in the dive bars lining the streets. At least not tonight. Muttering to myself as Tom Waits plays through my headphones. I take them off. Sometimes I just want to hear the sounds of the city streets.

Once again I sit in my apartment. Only the sound of a cabbie speeding up Sixth Avenue, running lights. Delivery men clanking chains on their bicycles, securing them to posts in the snow. The shades are open. The lamp is on. The reflecting light in the window makes the outside world invisible. I see only the bars through my reflection.

And my cat still sits in the other room.

11

Best friend from San Francisco in town for the weekend. Let's drink beer!

We always drank, playing card games. Tradition.

"Get the deck."

Looked everywhere. Couldn't find one. No way!

What to do? If no cards, how were we gonna play a game to drink the beer?

The deli on 14th street was my go-to spot. Deli, dollar store, and Kmart all rolled into one.

"What beer do they have? Coors, Miller, Bud, Corona?"

"They have everything, and I'm sure, playing cards."

"Get a 12 pack of Miller Lite."

"Hi, can I place an order for delivery?"

"Address?"

"334 East 14th street, apartment 5C."

"What can I get you?"

"Yeah, could I get two decks of playing cards?"

"Playing cards? No, we don't deliver that."

"Huh? Why not?"

"Look, we just don't. Quit wasting my time."

The line went dead. I stared at my phone. My friend laughed:

"Hey man, just call back and order the beer."

"Hi, can I place an order for delivery?"

"Address?"

"334 East 14th street, apartment 5C."

"What can I get you?"

"Can I get a 12 pack of Miller Lite?"

"Sure. Anything else?"

"And two decks of cards."

"Two decks of cards? You just called. I told you, I'm not delivering two decks of cards."

"Yeah, but you're gonna deliver the beer. Why can't you just slip the decks into the bag? It's not like I'm not going to pay for them."

My friend interrupted:

"Man, forget about the fucking cards. Just get the beer!"

"I'm not delivering the cards. I told you before, stop wasting my time!"

Click. The line went dead.

"Well? Are we getting the beer?"

"I dunno. How are we even gonna drink without the cards?"

5

Did I hear that right?

Walking west on 11th with my friend. Just had some beers. Head over to 3rd Avenue to meet with a few others. Sunny Saturday afternoon.

Each of us in our own gray worlds, we pass two girls. We hear one of them say:

"You should probably just kill yourself."

We both laugh.

"Do you think she was talking about me?"

"I don't know, maybe she was talking to me!"

"Weird shit, man."

Back in my gray world. Who was she talking about? Me?

Considering the literal meaning makes me uneasy.

Make it to 3rd Avenue. Round ordered. My friend repeats the phrase to the others. They all laugh; I display an uneasy smile.

Mind starts to spin. Can't let this go.

Maybe I should do it.
Why not?
Why bother being alive?
Was she right?
Why should I live?
Is the choice mine?
What does she think?

Feel nausea. Terror. Arbitrary.

Fuck it! Where's my drink?

7

We're just going to have a drink.

Hostess shows us to one of the many open tables.

Within a few moments the server comes over.

"What can I start you off with?"

I scan the menu. My girlfriend doesn't hesitate: "I'll have a gimlet."

I ask for a Stoli with soda and lime.

The server heads to the bar.

A busboy comes, places two glasses of water, napkins and silverware on our table. As I pick up my water, the uneven table wobbles, spilling my girlfriend's water. Gently, I place my foot on the table base to keep it stable.

The server returns, and as she sets our drinks down, she asks:

"Are you ready to order?"

"Oh, we're just having drinks."

"Sir, you can't sit at a table and only have drinks."

"We told the hostess we were only having drinks and she sat us here."

She immediately grabs the silverware and napkins and walks away.

Girlfriend picks up her gimlet and I feel the wobble again. I put my foot down harder on the base. She sees my irritation and mutters: "Just tell her to fix it."

"I'll see."

One small sip and she holds out her drink and eyes it suspiciously.

"This is awful. Did you try yours?"

I sip mine. "Yeah, this is pretty bad. Really weak."

"I'm going to say something. This is the worst gimlet I've ever had."

I squirm uncomfortably, but ensure my foot stays planted on the base of the table. She looks up toward the server and raises her hand: "Excuse me!"

I lean forward and lower my voice. "Can you please not say anything? Let's just finish these and get out of here."

She ignores me as the server comes over.

"These drinks are unacceptable. They don't have any alcohol, whatsoever."

I look down at the table, embarrassed. The server picks up each drink.

I look up: "What the hell? Why did you have to make such a fuss about it? It's really not that big a deal. Now we look ridiculous."

No response. A few silent minutes pass as she texts on her phone. I stare out the window.

My phone buzzes in my pocket. Text: "Why are u being such an asshole"

I blurt out, "Asshole?" as the server arrives at the table. The server looks at me and puts the drinks down.

As my girlfriend picks up her fresh drink, I lift my foot off the table base. The table wobbles, spilling her drink on her hand ever so slightly.

The drinks are practically pure alcohol, and judging by the way they burn, it's the cheap stuff.

Fuck it. I just want to get the check and get out. My girlfriend protests. "I just got my drink!"

"I don't care, let's get out of this dump, now."

The server passes by our table and I motion for the check.

I smile. "Thanks for re-doing the drinks."

She brings over the printed check. $21.31! A little note says suggested gratuity is %20. At the bottom a handwritten note:

Thank you! ☺ a.h.

3

Flying stresses me.

Dragging the bag around. Check in. Security. Shoes off. Belt off. Jacket off. Shoes on. Belt on. Jacket on. Run to the gate. Same routine.

This time I had to get to Europe for a wedding.

All started in a cab to JFK. Pulled up to the terminal. Handed the driver a couple twenties. Typically I run late. On this one occasion I had given myself plenty of time.

Squeezed my bag through the revolving door. Huge mass of people. No lines. No directions. No organization. Loudspeaker blasts:

"URGENT NOTICE: LUFTHANSA STRIKE. ALL FLIGHTS CANCELED."

Overwhelmed, I panic. Texted my girl:

"I'm afraid I'm not going to make it. There's a fucking strike."

She texted back reassurance:

"Everything will be OK. You're going to make it."

Made it through the chaos. Rebooked a seat on a British Airways flight. Time to spare. Had a few drinks. So glad she was there for me. The next two weeks were looking better.

Flight back from Europe was uneventful.

Called her from the cab. Heard her loving voice. I missed her. And I knew she missed me.

As we embraced, I was finally home.

Drowsy after the dinner she made me, we both fell into bed. Within a few minutes she was peacefully asleep in my arms. Whereas, I couldn't sleep, I gently eased myself out of bed. Watched TV for about an hour, some PBS special on supernovas, until I felt I could go to sleep.

Getting into bed, I noticed her phone lit up in the palm of her hand. I gently removed the phone to place it on her bedside table.

The message on her phone read:

"Yeah sleepin witu on saturday nite was the best nite of my life."

What the FUCK! What prompted this message?

The one above read:

"feeling you inside me was so amazing. I cantwait to do it again."

Replaced the phone in her hand, eased myself out of bed and left the apartment.

4

C heck my phone, 7:44. Hoping to get here earlier. No accident that I made sure to be the first to arrive.

The night is cool. There's a calm breeze; but, I'm sweating a little and my body feels like it's on fire.

Fidget on the barstool. Half sitting, half standing, I desperately try to catch the eye of the bartender. Why the fuck doesn't this fucking asshole notice me? Seeing his annoying bowtie makes me swallow.

"Maker's on the rocks." A nod.

The Mark comes with a glass of water and a bowl of nuts. I take a drink; stings my tongue. I ignore the water and pick at the almonds. The bartender nervously keeps a short-eye on me.

7:48. I have 12 minutes before the meeting. I push the ice around in the half-empty glass.

Is there enough time to have another Mark before she arrives? 7:52. The shaking has subsided a little bit, but my mind races, and I still feel beads of sweat on my forehead.

7:55. In front of me is the glass with half melted ice cubes. I nudge it away with the hope the bartender will notice my action. He doesn't. I see the door to the bar open. My heart skips a beat. I feel a wave of heat and dread go through my body from head to toe. Not her.

What is this bartender, this bowtied idiot doing? Why won't he respond to me? Maybe that bowtie is cutting off the blood supply to his brain. I feel like screaming.

Finally, I motion for another round. He takes his sweet time. Come on, come on, come on! I'm too frightened to check the time. Bowtie moves quicker, maybe sensing my agitation. He pours the Maker's. He picks up the empty glass and replaces it with the full one. I down it in one swallow.

The world seems serene. Wonder if I should have brought my light jacket with me. The evenings can be quite chilly.

The door opens. There she is, 8:00. Right on the mark. She gives me a hug. I'm unresponsive; I don't say a word. Without even ordering a drink, she begins complaining about work. I stare at my empty glass.

"I saw your phone last night."

"What?"

"I fucking saw everything! You and me, we're finished."

19

The wedding was the first event I had been to since it happened.

Months had passed. It was hard finding out my fiancée had been having an affair. She walked out on me. We had been together for so long.

Moved into a new building right after it happened. A new life. My neighbor, Kelly, was a sweet girl who had helped me get acquainted with the neighborhood. I figured, what the hell, I'd ask Kelly to accompany me to the wedding. She happily obliged.

My ex and I had a lot of mutual friends. They were all there.

As an EMT, my friends were always interested on how my shifts went. They asked me about my previous night. Some college kid smoked a bunch of pot. He heard sirens outside his apartment, freaked, and called 911. We got the call: a man, drugs, thought he was dying.

"Well, was he dying?"

"No, he was totally fine." I laughed.

I went through proper protocols. Did his basic evaluation. Baseline vitals. Medical history. Contact information. I asked who I should call.

He wanted his girlfriend. No family. I called her and informed her we would be at St. George's.

ER was busy. Long wait. As time went by this kid's high went down. He realized he wasn't dying, and got agitated. He wanted to go home, but I told him that we had already started the paperwork, so he couldn't leave. He got belligerent and cursed at me. Now I was pissed. This asshole had smoked too much weed, took up my time, and now wanted to bitch about it. By now my friends were laughing.

When the intake nurse finally called us, I handed her the paperwork. Suddenly my patient cheered up. His girlfriend walked in. She came and hugged him and took his hand. It annoyed me. I told the nurse what the complaint was:

"This douche bag idiot smoked too much weed and thought he was about to die. Moron."

Kelly looked at me.

"You actually said that?"

"Yeah, that's exactly what I said."

My friends laughed even louder.

The patient looked down when I said that. So did his girlfriend. When we put him in the corner bed in the ER, he turned and faced the wall. The girlfriend asked me:

"Is he OK?"

I barely looked at her.

"Yeah, fine."

After a few moments, Kelly politely excused herself to use the bathroom. One of my friends turned to me:

"Hey man, it's great to see you out again, with a new girl."

"Kelly is just my neighbor."

"Even so. You know we saw your ex last weekend."

"Huh?"

"Yeah, she just showed up to Vanessa's birthday party with some guy. We were all surprised to see her. I couldn't believe she had the nerve to show up with a guy after what she did to you. She tried to include herself in our conversation, but we all turned away, she ran out of the bar in tears, obviously humiliated."

I nodded. Went to get a new drink.

As I stood at the bar, I imagined my ex in tears running out of that party.

Then I thought about my patient, facing the wall, with his girlfriend holding his hand.

How did this all begin?

17

B ut it's going to be there forever.

"How will you feel tomorrow? The day after that? Years from now? It will always be a mark on you. Even in your mind."

No. I'm going to love it. It'll be great. I'm going there tonight. As soon as I finish with this exam.

I'm a sophomore in college. I can do what I want. I can get a tattoo. I'll just do it. Tonight. But now I gotta take this quiz in my Roman antiquities class. Pompeii. Shit, back then I would've had a whole family at my age. A wife. Kids. My mom can't tell me what to do anymore. They can't control me. I do what I want. I can make my own rules.

Would my life be so dramatically altered in a single act? Forever?

I scribbled my name on the top of the quiz, and got right to the first question:

A photo of heavily dust covered bodies, petrified. In contorted positions. Obviously the result of some kind of disaster.

1.) In what year did Mt. Vesuvius erupt, collapsing buildings, and killing roughly 2,000 people?

A.) 55 B.C.

B.) 323 B.C.

C.) 79 A.D.

D.) 13150 B.C.

Clearly "C." I breezed through the rest.

Handed in my exam. "Everything all good professor?"

After a glance: "Yup, looks fine. Just write down the date."

"Oops sorry."

I scribbled down the date.

Monday, September 10, 2001.

10

Anthony Marek, from my wildlife law class, got arrested last night for soliciting sex from a child.

Oh shit! Gotta print out my outline for that class. First final exam of second year law. Hafta get through this day.

I'm already late. Okay, wildlife cases that'll be on the test. Start the car. Birds, mammals, anything else? Radio.

"Two people were shot early this morning in McKees Rocks. Police are currently invest..." Get off! What appellate court was the Migratory Bird Treaty Act involved in? 8th? 9th?

Did I lock the car? Stupid first class: International Business Transactions.

"Ok everyone, Hilton v. Guyot. Let's start with the background. This was the last case involving foreign..."

Marine Mammal Protection Act. That's going to be on the test. Damn. Manatees in Florida, yeah. Have to know this. Gotta get an A on the exam.

"...and don't forget to study US taxation of overseas operations for the final. I'll see you all on Monday." Shit! Do I have time for lunch?

"Yeah I'll, have a turkey on rye, lettuce, tomato, mustard." I love this deli. Need to flip through the outline again. "No, no, mustard, not mayo."

I'm sure there's something about fish in Tennessee. Why is my phone buzzing? Text: "Don't forget to wish dad happy birthday."

I know, I know. His sister died a few weeks ago. Were the salmon streaming downstream or upstream in the Pacific Northwest? Damn!

"Ok class, last week we talked about fair use. Who can start us off on..." Copyright Law.

Shit, did I check the most recent decision on the Pennsylvania Wildlife and Fish statutes? Hafta get the local paper. Stupid headlines:

3 U.S. marines killed by an IED in Afghanistan.

Pitt Law student arrested for underage solicitation.

Eritrea famine; thousands feared dead; bodies stacked outside doors.

Court rules in favor of trappers against Pennsylvania Fish and Wildlife Dept.

Great. That's what I needed. Hope it's on the test. Why is my phone buzzing again? "missed call Dad". Make sure porpoises were covered by the Marine Mammal Protection Act. Damn, the birds too! Only 25 minutes before I have to go inside and take the test. The fucking noise from the ambulance. Oh, here it is on page 12. Yeah, porpoises are covered.

Hot and stuffy in here. Just hand out the test already! Oh yeah, he said the Chevron case wasn't going to be on the exam.

"Hey did you hear about Anthony Marek?"

"What?" I don't even know this girl across the aisle.

"He got arrested yesterday."

"Oh, yeah. I saw that." Hell, it's hot in here...it's really hot.

"Anthony Marek. Did you think he was a perp?"

"I don't know!" ...I don't know.

Anthony Marek. - Anthony, a real person. I knew him. His life is destroyed!

"Okay class, you have two hours..."

24

D amn. Pharmacy closes at 5.

Gotta get through Union Square and Washington Square. Gonna be crowded.

Headphones on. Insulation from what's around me.

Head down as I enter Union Square. They're all around me. It begins.

Repent now and accept Jesus as your savior or burn in hell for eternity!

Hare Hare Hare Hare Krishna! Join us!

Join us against Zionism! We demand a Palestinian state!

Don't you have time for Greenpeace? Don't you want so save the world?

Hey man, let's play! You can take first move. But your queen is my bitch!

Out the square, down 5th Avenue. Then to Washington.

First sign:

homeless pregnant and HIV +.

Semper Fi. Need help. Vet.

"Hey man, you want some we...."

I gotta get through this. Signs everywhere. Songs for money. Acrobats.

At pharmacy. 4:53 P.M. Old lady in front front of me, at the counter:

"I'm sorry sir, just how much is a Hershey bar?"

"Its 2.99"

"Are you sure?"

"Yes, Ma'am."

"You know, it used you be fifty-nine cents." Took out a small change purse.

Feebly shelled out. Inspected nickels and dimes.

Are you kidding me? I felt I was about to lose it. I rolled my eyes. Come on, come on!

"What can I do for you, sir?"

"I called in a script half hour ago."

"Name?"

"Johnson, Mary."

Back in Washington Square. iPod dead. Pull off headphones.

Weed, weed, weed!

Dude, help a starving musician!

Union Square. Save the whales!

Christ will save you!

This time I yell back: "Why doesn't Christ save the whales? Eliminate the middleman!" I wasn't noticed.

Go forward.

Kid in a blue shirt with a clipboard: "Do you have a second to save a child's life? Just a few dollars a month?"

"Out of my way, asshole."

"Selfish Prick." The kid mutters.

"WHAT? I'm the selfish prick? What the FUCK do you know about saving a child? I shove the bag in his face. "This'll save a child!"

8

She thought she was a social butterfly, the center of attention. The fact is she was just a drunk who would get so blitzed she would talk to any stranger. It bothered me.

It was a typical Saturday night. Knew what to expect. She would get belligerent at the end and pass out. I'd have to get her home and struggle to get her out of the cab. Essentially, I would end up being the chaperone. Why did I do it?

She had a friend who was having a birthday celebration that night. I had a few things to catch up on, so I planned to meet her after I finished. She told me the name of the place they were meeting.

When I arrived, she wasn't there. I double checked, I had the right place. Texted: "Where are you?" No response. After waiting 10 minutes in a nearby doorway, she texted. She had given me the wrong place. She told me where they were. Annoyed, got into a cab.

I arrived to find a 30 minute wait line to get in the club. It was a cold January night. God damn it! This time I called. "Just suck it up and wait in line!"

What the fuck!

Resigned to my fate, once inside the deafening chaos of the club, I texted: "Can you come to the front and bring me to your table?"

After too long, she appeared out of the crowd and blurted out:

"You know what, just leave! I don't even want you here!" "Um, why!?"

"Because you have a bad attitude and I don't want you to be around my friends!"

I just looked at her. She turned and disappeared back into the crowd.

Outside, the freezing air and a gust of wind kicked me awake. I huddled, pulling my jacket tighter across my chest and stared at the concrete in front of me. The street was filled with loud drunk college kids.

Gotta go home. Left foot, same concrete. Right foot, same concrete. What the fuck just happened? Why am I doing all this? What am I?

My key in the latch. Who the fuck does that girl think she is? What the fuck did I do? I paced around my apartment in circles, my mind racing. Screw her! Gotta get some sleep. Headphones and got in bed. The rhythm of the music sucked me into a deathly sleep.

Don't hear from her the next morning. Not in the afternoon. I finally relented and called her cell. Voicemail. "I hope you're all right."

By late afternoon, I checked my email and found her online: "What's going on." Her fury unleashed: "I SHOULD BREAK UP WITH YOU RIGHT NOW. YOU DON'T EVEN KNOW WHAT HAPPENED LAST NIGHT."

Panic! "What? What happened?"

"I LOST MY BAG THAT HAD MY PHONE, KEYS, AND WALLET. THEN I CAME OVER TO YOUR APARTMENT AND

WAS SLAMMING ON YOUR DOOR. WHERE WERE YOU?? OUT WITH A HOOKER YOU ASSHOLE?"

"I was home, you know I'm a heavy sleeper."

"Whatever, FUCK YOU. YOU BETTER COME OVER HERE AND BEG FOR FORGIVENESS."

Fuck her! I am done with this crazy bitch! I slammed the door as I began preparing my apology.

9

G et out! We're through! This time, I really mean it! Was she for real this time? I left her apartment, and started the walk back home on that warm New York Sunday evening.

A little panic. Took a deep breath and tried to clear my mind. I decided this was just another one of her threats. Once home, checked on the cat, looked in the fridge, switched on the TV. Poured a small bourbon. I started an old movie. When it ended, got into bed. On nights like these we usually went out to Eddies, a local bar. Last time we were there she struck up a long conversation with the bartender. Was she doing that tonight?

Next morning I decided to go to the park and sit outside to do some writing. I checked my phone before heading out: no calls, no messages from her.

Despite the fact it was a Monday there was a lively crowd. Musicians, performers, kids wading in the fountain. I got into my writing. That evening would have been pleasant, except she wasn't there.

Tuesday I had some errands and appointments. That evening I met up with an old friend. Couldn't help bring up my fears about what might be happening between her and me. I kept checking my phone hoping to see a message from her.

She must have been out. Later, I drank at home just to lessen the obsessing, but it only got worse. Had I really lost her? Was she out screwing around? Had she gotten over me already?

I woke up Wednesday hung-over believing she was really gone. That day was a waste. I couldn't even write. In the evening I decided to go to out to a little hole in the wall bar not too far from my apartment. I carried my notebook with me in hopes I might be able to write. Finally went back to my apartment. She hadn't contacted me since I left her place on Sunday night. I guessed that was it. It was just then I heard my phone vibrate. It was her. I answered. It was difficult to hear her, lot of background noise of a bar:

"I feel so sick. I have to come over, now!"

Shortly thereafter, my doorbell rang. As I opened the door she pushed right past me and fell onto the couch. "If you had been there this wouldn't have happened to me!", and she passed out. Put her to bed. Things back to normal.

In the morning I woke her and asked if she were going to work. Mumbled she was feeling too sick and would just call in late. I got up and cleaned my apartment. She finally got up around noon.

"Are you feeling better?"

"Eh."

"You feel ok to go to work now?"

"Are you fucking kicking me out?"

That evening I got a text from her: "Hey I'm meeting up with some friends tonight. U wanna join?"

"I thought you were feeling sick?"

"No I'm fine."

When I arrived at the bar, she was already pretty drunk. After a short time it was clear she had to go home. Got her into a cab. We were there in 5 minutes. Got her safely to bed. I turned to leave and she shouted: "Fuck you. Why didn't you take me back to your place! You're just gonna leave me here, alone?"

"It's for the best," as I left her apartment.

Friday morning I saw a message on my phone: "I was going to invite you to go bowling tonight but after last night, we are through!"

I didn't respond. That evening, headed to a bar. There was a soccer match I wanted to watch and I was hoping to do some writing anyway.

When I got to the bar, I took the first seat available. Ordered a beer. Kept my eye on the TV but opened my notebook.

At a key moment in the match a girl next to me yelled: "What the hell was that? That's bullshit! That's not a penalty!"

I smiled. "Yeah I agree, that was a total dive in the box." We kept laughing and agreeing through the rest of the first half. Watching games with my girlfriend usually ended in a fight.

At half time she asked me: "Hey, I'm gonna go to another bar to watch the second half of the game. I know the bartender there. You wanna go?"

"Sure."

At the next bar we sat at a table near the entrance with a good view of the TV. Suddenly I saw her, walking toward me. I thought she was going bowling that night. As she passed the table, glaring at me she muttered: "Some new bitch already, huh?" Then she walked out the door.

"Excuse me, I have to deal with this."

She had just lit a cigarette. "What are you doing with that bitch?"

"It's just someone I met watching the game."

"And you have to show up here and throw it in my face? Why didn't you have the balls to tell me we're finished!?"

"We are."

"How can you abandon me like this when you know how much I need you?"

I just stared at her.

"FUCK YOU!," as she turned away.

I watched her walk toward the end of the block, she didn't look back once. Before she made it to the corner she stopped, sat down on the curb between two parked cars and put her face in her hands, sobbing.

I took a step toward her, then stopped. I turned to walk home. About a block away I wiped tears from my eyes.

18

Oh my God, I kissed another girl!

Friday night I was to meet my girlfriend after work to celebrate her promotion. Enough time to meet friends for a drink before.

Crowded bar. After a few drinks, lost track of time. Head downstairs to the toilet.

Two lines. Next to me is a girl slowly rocking back and forth. She looks at me: "I hope this one won't take long, I really need to pee," gesturing toward the door.

I respond, "Yeah, me too. Like a racehorse."

Her door opens first, and she bolts in. Mine opens a moment later.

Done. So is she. As we both head up the stairs, she turns:

"See ya around."

At the top of the stairs I gently touch her hand. She turns. Our lips meet.

Oh my God, I kissed another girl!

Oh my God, I'm late. Out the door into a cab.

I see her as soon as I walk in. She looks agitated. Oh my God, does she know I kissed that girl?

"What happened, why are you so late?"

"Uh, I had to help this girl. She was passed out on the floor where I met my friends. You know I have EMT training. Had to wait for an ambulance to arrive."

Shit. She's not going to believe that.

"Oh, ok, you gave her the kiss of life," she laughs.

"What do you mean the kiss of life?"

She's playing with me, she knows.

"Well isn't that what they call it when you do artificial respiration?"

"Yeah, but why would you say that?"

"Look, I thought we were here to celebrate. I'm just saying you did a sweet thing, helping that girl."

"Anybody would have done it. Anyway, tell me about the promotion."

"Well, my manager called me in about 10 a.m. and…"

Thank God she doesn't get it.

"…you know the one who had the affair?"

Oh shit, she's setting me up. "Well was that ever proven?"

"I don't know, anyway, he told me I had been doing such a great job he wanted to show me something."

Oh, yeah I'll bet he wanted to show her something, that asshole. I know what I would show her.

"That's when he presented me with my promotion."

I just stare at her.

"Aren't you happy for me?"

"Of course, I knew you would get promoted."

"You're so sweet."

She smiles, puts a reassuring hand on my cheek and gives me a small kiss.

"I guess she wore cherry chapstick?"

She knows.

6

A hot summer night up at the cabin. Needed a little time on my own.

Feet propped up on the porch railing, I sipped a beer and looked down at the dark waters of the natural harbor below.

I needed time at the cabin because I had been given an ultimatum.

I took another drink and watched moths frantically dance around the hot porch light.

I did not want to make any decision.

I put the half empty beer down, walked to the beach, stepped into the small dinghy and shoved off. I turned and started the out board motor. Before turning around, I stared at that porch light.

I looked forward into the darkness, the ocean beyond.

The soft purring of the motor was the only sound in the night. Again, I turned to see the porch light. Then I turned back into the darkness, everything felt right.

The water gently slapped the boat as I motored on. I turned to see the porch light; then once again back into the darkness.

By now, the sound of the motor was drowned out by louder slapping waves. I nervously turned to see the porch light.

It was gone.

Knowing the light had been behind me, I reached back to turn the motor reversing course. I motored for a while, but still no light. I desperately screamed for help.

After a few moments the porch light appeared to my right. Relieved, I headed the bow of the dinghy toward the light.

Suddenly, another light appeared to my left. And another. And another. Then more to my right. I was surrounded by countless shimmering lights frantically dancing around the dinghy.

I cut the engine. Leaned over the side of the boat and scooped up a handful of the shimmering light. It was nothing but phosphorescent fish.

I slumped back in the boat. These deceivers were not going to guide me home. There was no porch light.

There was no ultimatum.

14

I had never seen a grown man cry like that.

Steamy, quiet Brooklyn night. Too hot to cut the ambulance's engine. We needed the air conditioning. I listened to the dispatch radio while my partner snoozed. Quiet. We waited in the McDonald's parking lot, bored.

1:04 a.m:

"Four-zero Charlie for the assignment, four-zero Charlie."

"Four-zero Charlie," I responded.

"Four-zero Charlie, 4102 5th Avenue for the unconscious," crackled back.

"Ten-four, send info."

Saw the information come up on the central console monitor: "Man reports finding six year old daughter not breathing."

"Four-zero Charlie, ten-sixty three. On our way."

My partner jostled awake as I pulled out of the lot and flipped on the emergency lights. Empty streets.

"Four-zero Charlie, double eight. On scene."

Grabbed the oxygen tank and the defibrillator. My partner got the trauma kit.

Front door flew open before we reached the stairs. The flashing emergency lights hit his face, on, off, on, off. Draped across his arms was the limp body of the girl. There, not there, there, not there.

We asked him to put her down, and began to work on her. Breathing shallow. Rapid heart rate. Low blood pressure. Bad signs. Oxygen straight away.

"This ever happen to her before?"

"Yeah, but not this bad." Father breathing heavily.

I looked up. "Any explanation?"

"She's got advanced sickle cell."

Damn it.

Her vitals continued to deteriorate. Running out of time. No time for the stretcher, I carried her into the ambulance while my partner kept working on her. Her father got in, I could see the terror on his face. Jumped in the driver seat, blasted the sirens.

Just a few minutes to the emergency room. I keyed my radio:

"Four-zero Charlie."

"Four-zero Charlie go."

"Four zero Charlie, ten-eighty two. We need notification. Lutheran Hospital. 6 year old female, severe respiratory and cardiac distress."

"Ten-four."

The hospital would be ready for her when we arrived. I heard my partner yell out:

"Slow down. CPR."

Fuck. She had stopped breathing. There was no pulse. Can't do CPR in a fast moving vehicle. I slowed a bit. Almost there.

The ER doctor and several nurses were waiting. We gave them all the information we could. My partner and I continued CPR as they got to work on her.

After 10 minutes, the monitors showed no sign of life. At 1:33 a.m. the doctor told us to cease CPR. She was declared dead.

He had been kept aside while we worked, but he could see that we had all stopped treating her. He just lost it, screaming and crying and hitting himself. It took three police officers in the ER just to restrain him. Three grown men. Suddenly the only sound in the ER was the scream of this little girl's name by her father, while two of the cops wept.

In 29 minutes my night had gone from boring to the death of a 6 year old girl.

Ran to a bathroom. Locked the door. Vomited my guts out.

My partner and I began our routine of getting our unit available again: replaced the stretcher bedding, replaced the non-rebreather oxygen mask, and made sure our paperwork was complete.

"Four-zero Charlie for the assignment, four-zero Charlie."

"Four-zero Charlie, here."

15

H ey!

"HEY!"

Ignored it. The bar is half a block away.

"HEEEYYY!"

Now I was pissed. What the hell does this girl want? I turned:

"What do you WANT?"

"Do you have a cigarette I could borrow?"

I just stared at her for a moment.

"What? No! I don't smoke."

"Oh ok, thanks! Have a nice night!"

She smiled.

Irritated, I walked into the bar.

An hour and a couple of pints. A little writing. Bored. Left.

Back out on the street:

"Hey!"

She was in my face.

"Hey, do you have a cigarette?"

"Really? What's your deal? You just asked me an hour ago. I don't smoke. Ask someone else."

She put her face in her hands and sobbed.

"Hey, hey, what's wrong?"

"My cat, my cat. Last night my boyfriend broke up with me and I don't know what to do. Where do I go? My cat. He has my cat. Oh my God can you please help me?"

"I don't think there's anything I can do for you."

She pointed right across the street, at a tenement. "I can't reach the fire escape ladder. Could you just pull it down for me? I gotta get my cat."

"Ok but that's it."

We crossed Horatio Street. I caught the ladder on the third jump.

"OK, I'm gonna go."

"I can't do this. I'm afraid."

Again with the sobbing.

"Can you please, please do this for me? She's an orange tabby cat. She's a rescue cat. She depends on me."

"Look I got things to do. I have to go."

"I'm begging you. Her name is Cringer. She has a red collar. Please."

I looked up at the fire escape. I knew this was a bad idea as I started climbing.

"It's the third floor on the right."

I put my back against the outside wall right next to the window she was pointing at. It was slightly open. I looked back down and saw the girl looking up at me. What the hell was I doing? I could feel it beginning to drizzle. Snuck a peek through the edge of the window:

Holy shit. Guy on top of a girl. Both naked. He was fucking her. Legs in the air. I froze.

A second later, an orange cat, red collar, jumped up on the indoor windowsill with a slight ring of the bell on the collar. I didn't think. I pushed up the window. "Come on Cringer!" I grabbed her collar and scooped her into the crook of my right arm.

The girl in the apartment screamed:

"WHAT THE FUCK?"

Cringer hissed. Claws into me. "SHIT!"

She was shredding my shirt. Her collar kept jingling. I slipped several times on the wet rungs of the fire escape, saved only by my free left hand.

"TAKE YOUR CAT!"

I slipped the last 2 rungs and fell on the pavement, still clutching the cat.

The girl was gone.

"YOU MOTHERFUCK PIECE OF SHIT PRICK! IM

GOING TO FUCKIN' BUST YOU UP!"

I looked up. Naked guy leaning over the fire escape. Oh shit. Shit, shit, shit.

I ran. Cringer continued to shred my skin. Howls. Had to get out of there. I reached the corner and looked back. Naked guy climbing down the ladder, yelling, coming after me.

"CRINGER, STOP FUCKING SCRATCHING ME!"

"Hey!"

12

I press down firmly on her neck and back. I've done this many times as an EMT. She struggles and I press down harder. I'm shaking, or maybe she is. She's clearly in pain. The tech carefully inserts the needle into her leg. Within seconds, I feel her muscles begin to relax. Tension eases. I slowly take my hands off her body and I feel my fear set in. I go back out to the waiting room.

I flash back.

"Mommy, mommy! Can I please have him?"

Oh wow! My first pet! He scrambles around his cage, nervous, frantic. I love him! Every night he runs on his wheel. I really like the squeaky sound it makes. It helps me to sleep. I'm always good about feeding him. I need my dad to help me change the litter in his cage though. He's so cool! I think we are really starting to get along now. He lets me pick him up!

"Mommy, mommy! He got out!"

"What do you mean?"

"He's not in his cage!"

"It's ok, we'll find him."

Oh no. I left the latch off the top of his cage. He got out. He's gone. I lost him. I cry and sniffle. This is the worst day of my life.

"We need you to come to the surgery room. She's still asleep, but the doctor would like to speak with you."

Sweat runs down my forehead. Hands shake. The doctor stands there, motionless. "The surgery was complicated but went well. You'll have to wait awhile for the anesthesia to wear off."

Back to the waiting area. Wish I could get out of here.

"Mommy. I can't find him."

He's nowhere to be found. I'm scared. Mommy comes into my room as I search behind my desk.

"It's bedtime. We will look more tomorrow."

I can't sleep. I cry. I miss the squeaking sound of his wheel.

The next day in school we're doing multiplication tables, but all I can think about is my pet.

I get home, and I ask mommy if she's found him.

"No, honey."

I run up the stairs to my room. I drop my backpack on the floor and there he is, sitting in the middle of my pile of stuffed animals! I can't believe it. I slowly approach, and gently cradle him.

"Mommy, mommy! I found him! He's ok!"

"Sir. Sir? She's ready to go home now. You'll need to monitor her very carefully overnight. You can come and pick her up."

See her laying on the table. She looks weak. I'm still shaking, but try to reassure her with a stroke of her fur.

I pick her up, gently cradle her. She purrs lightly, and gives me a slight lick on my hand.

Relief.

16

F riday afternoon. Party that night. East Village.

Boyfriend driving down from med school.

Crossed Washington Square Park. She and her roommate headed to their apartment.

She tossed a dime and a few pennies into a blue paper coffee cup. Accompanying that cup, a leaf encrusted lost human.

Roommate laughed: "Why did you give money to that druggie?"

"I dunno, still don't get why they just don't at least get a job at McDonald's or something. They're pathetic."

Smart, taller, older. Med school boyfriend waiting in lobby.

Bedroom door closed. He licked the back of her neck. She blushed as she put on her brand new blouse.

Cab door closed. 1st Avenue.

Apartment door opens. Volume high. Booze flows.

"Wow, who's the boyfriend?"

After some drinks, they sit. Casual conversation.

"Hey!" Med school boyfriend holds out a packet. "You wanna try this? It's some hot shit."

Several takers. She hesitates.

"You gonna miss out?"

"No, screw it. Pass it over."

K2'd.

"Hey girlie, you OK? You been standin' there a while just starin' at that M&M sign. You OK?"

Flashing bright lights, hands on pavement, surrounded by thousands of nightmare faces. Throw up.

It's dark. Sick. Shouts and sirens. "Malcolm what Boulevard?" A toothless grin in her face:

"Hey there young lady. You don't look so good. You ok?"

"What?"

"You ok? You need something? Come with me honey. I gotcha."

"Water."

"Here honey, drink this, it'll make you feel better."

"It burns. Water?"

"Honey, this is better than water."

"Leave me alone!"

Black forest. Tall buildings. Wet grass. So tired.

4 a.m. Gotta switch from night manager to day manager at McDonald's. Glad to be home. Just wanna sleep.

Ah, shit. Those fuckin' homeless people always sleeping in my doorway. "Hey, you gotta move, you can't sleep here. We're just a few blocks from Washington Square. Go crash there." She's pretty well dressed to be homeless.

"Water."

"Ok, but ya gotta move."

I'll just give her some water in one of my red plastic cups.

Back down. She chugged it and tried to hand it back.

"No, no, keep it for next time. You'll need it. Take it easy."

"No, wait!"

13

O h my God, my dick!

Never been to East Berlin before. Only thing I know about Germany is beer comes by the liter.

First night. Don't know where to go, what to do. Hell, let me just go get my first liter!

Streets are dark. Some suspicious faces.

Enter the first bar I find. Its dark, and the wooden furnishings smell like they've been marinating in alcohol for the last 30 years. Take a seat. Bartender looks at me. "Uh, beer?"

He turns, without a word, and starts to pour with precise efficiency. Suddenly to my left:

"Amerikanisch!"

He's a big, brawny guy, clearly downed a couple. He stumbles over with his liter and plops down on the stool next to me. He immediately wraps my shoulder with a black smith's arm.

"Von wo kommst du? Uh, where from? Chi-cago? Michael Jordan! Bang, bang!"

I smile politely.

"No, no, I am from New York."

"Ohhh, Times Squares! Girlies!"

He takes out a wad of cash and slams it on the bar as the bartender gives me my beer. Seems like I've made a friend already!

"Willkommen! Prost!"

We exchange as much conversation as we can. I try to find out what to do in Berlin. He tries to find out what to do in "Times Squares."

"Mehr bier!"

Before I know it, I'm done with my liter and I'm buying the next round. Then suddenly a third round. I'm really feeling it now.

"Deutsche und Amerikanishen, gut friend! Gut, gut, gut!"

"Ja, ja, ja!", showing off my drunken German speaking abilities.

He gives me a slap on my back and stands up.

"Ich muss pissen!"

I don't know exactly what he means, but he wanders off with his beer. I stare off into space, content with my new Berliner friend. What a nice, jovial guy!

He returns after a few minutes. But doesn't come back to the bar. He sits on a musty old couch and waves me over.

"Meine freundin, her kommen!" as he slaps his leg,

I happily stumble over to him, liter in hand. As soon as I reach him, he grabs me by the waist and pulls me down, right into his lap, side saddle. Maybe this is some kind of way Germans hang out? Bizarre. I don't think too much of it, probably because I'm inebriated.

"Men we are together! We drink beer!" He takes a swig of his beer, sets it down, and with that, he grabs my head with both hands and plants a kiss on my cheek. Ok, now this is getting pretty weird. I try to convince myself this is some kind of Berlin custom, but I really don't know.

It took a moment for me to actually process it. But sure enough, this guy has reached round my waist and has grabbed my dick, over my jeans. Here I am, East Berlin, in some shady bar, and now some stranger who I met an hour ago is holding my dick. Holy shit.

I try to push his hand away but he won't budge. I don't want to be too forceful, after all, my dick and my life are literally in his hands. He has latched onto me.

"Meine freundin!"

I nervously nod. I gotta get out of this! Jesus! I manage to stand up, but he still won't let go. So now I'm standing in this bar and this guy is just sitting there holding my dick. This is ridiculous. What the hell is he doing?

In desperation, I see he has no more beer.

I point. "Beer!"

He looks at his glass and releases.

I casually walk to the bar, then run for the door.

Oh my God, my dick!

21

I really like him. He's the first guy who has expressed his feeling toward me. He may be the one!

U should be careful. U just saw ur ex last week

I kno but i really like this guy

K hun, luv U

...

Hows it goin with dat chick?

Shes a total skank!

Lol, she that good in bed?

Complete ho. Luv it.

haha how long is this gonna last

Lets just say this isn't the kinda girl you bring home to your mom

Lol got it

...

I saw those shit things you wrote about me to ur friend.

What are you talking about?

So you cant bring me home to ur mom huh

That was just a joke

So im a joke??

I didn't mean it. You know how much I care about you, u gotta believe me

Fuck u don't message me anymore

I'm really sorry. Please. Ill do anything to make it up to

You

Fuck u. You're a liar

I would do anything for you, you know that.

What can you possibly do to fix this?

Anything.

So you would even marry me?

Yeah

Are you serious

Of course.

Yeah right.

No I swear.

I dunno. I need time

...

Are you serious? He said he would marry you after all the

shit he wrote?

I know hes full of shit. He wont go through with it.

You would even consider it?

but he might be the one...

...

She saw our texts

oh damn, even you calling her a skank?

gotta try to get her back

lol why do you want her

I really like her. Shes fun and great in bed

Youre fucked

I might marry her.

...

So we're set

Yea, ill pick u up at 8:30, we will be at city hall by 9

...

It had been five years since I heard from my friend. He was in town for business. Already on my second beer when he walked in.

"Hey buddy, how ya been?"

We caught up. Then he asked.

"So how's the wife?"

"We divorced after a year. Found out she was having an affair with her ex-boyfriend."

20

Hey we got a whale here. We can't move him ourselves. You guys down to assist? crackled the radio.

"That bad, huh? Send me the address."

I turned to my partner: "Fuck man, these whale calls are a killer on my back." I flipped on the siren and we were off.

"God damn! This guy's a big one! Must be 350 or more! What do you think Jimmy?"

"When was the last time he even got out of bed?" Jimmy laughingly asked. We all laughed.

"Hey guys I'm really hurting. Can you give me something for the pain?" groaned the fat man.

"Will the stretcher even hold him?" whined my partner.

"Damn man, should we call another unit?" muttered Jimmy.

"Shit, I hate these calls."

"Guys, please. I'm really in pain here. I really need something," pleaded the fat man.

"Man and I thought my neighbor Angelique was a pig!"

"Hey, didn't you bang her couple of times?" More laughter.

"Thank God this is the last call of the shift. Let's get rid of this one as fast as we can," as I flipped on the siren and floored it.

"Guys, it's gonna be awhile before the doc gets here," the nurse said as she exited the examining room.

"Ah shit, how long are we gonna have to hang around here?"

The fat man shifted uncomfortably: "Guys, I have a problem."

"Let's just go get started on the paperwork."

We all turned toward the door. As we walked out, the fat man grabbed my arm. I instinctively attempted to pull away.

"I really have a problem."

"What?"

"My…my private parts are stuck."

"Huh?"

"They're stuck between my legs. I can't reach them. I need you to adjust them. Please. I'm sorry."

I strapped on a fresh pair of latex gloves.

I ripped the sheet off, threw it on a chair, exposed his nude body.

I dug between his fleshy thighs. This was more difficult than I would have imagined. My fingers searchingly pried around.

Just then I heard a whimper. I looked over at the fat man's face. He had turned away and quietly sobbed.

The sobbing became louder and I saw him put his hands over his face. I fixed the problem.

I took the sheet from the chair, and gently laid it over him, ensuring he was covered. I placed my hand on his shoulder for a moment, and hesitated. I left the room.

Shift done. Local bar. The four of us.

"Hey man, what the fuck were you doing in there with the fat man after we left? What, you give him a hand job?"

"No, no, no! You gave him a blowjob! Shit, can you imagine trying to find his dick in that fat?"

"Yeah man, so what happened? You get his number?"

I just sipped my beer and looked away.

"Come on man, what was it? Hand or mouth?", Jimmy slapped my shoulder.

"No, no, you gotta spill it bro. You like your guys fat? Why so quiet?"

"Ohhhh, he liked it!"

"Come on Bryan, what the fuck happened?"

I calmly pushed my chair from the table, stood up, and walked out.

23

M an, what are we gonna do tonight? I know it's not the weekend yet, but we gotta celebrate our Freshman year of college!

My roommate taps at his computer. Turns: "Let's just do some poker. Be easy."

"Who we gonna get?"

"Frankie down the hall?"

"Frankie? Seriously? That kid has a pig in his dorm room. What's his name? Vladimir?"

"Whatever. Let's at least get Frankie and we'll find a fourth."

I knock on his door. Frankie answers. "We're playing poker. You wanna sit in?"

"Sure, let me get Vladimir."

"Really? Do we have to include him? He shits everywhere!"

"Come on man, you're gonna hurt his feelings."

I mutter to my roommate: "I can't believe he's bringing Vladimir."

"Well, he can be the fourth player," he says laughingly, "maybe we can still find someone else."

"Let's go to the common room. I'm dealing." Roommate to my left. Frankie to the right. Vladimir sits across from me.

"We playing with the same rules, fellas? Shot of booze for a lost hand?"

"Yeah especially if we are playing with a pig, we'll need a lot of bourbon," my roommate sarcastically mutters under his breath. Frankie shoots him a glance:

Vlad's is a great poker player, man. Taught him myself.

Watch."

My first hand is shit. Frankie flips over Vladimir's cards. Straight. Vlad wins. We losers take a shot.

My second hand is shit. Frankie leans over to Vladimir and whispers something inaudible. He looks at me: "Vladimir wants three cards. I'll take one myself."

"Are you serious, man?" I deal Vlad three new ones. He squeals.

Second hand goes to Vladimir again. A flush! "You see man? I told you he knows how to play."

"This is so dumb man." Vladimir grunts.

I win the third hand, but fourth and fifth once again go to Vladimir.

Frankie pushes himself from the table. "Man, I think I gotta piss. How about you Vladimir?" Frankie stands up. Vladimir relieves himself right there.

"DUDE WHAT THE FUCK! I AIN'T CLEANING

THAT!" I say angrily.

"Vladimir is fuckin' killin' us in poker." my roommate whispers to me.

"Round six!" as Frankie stumbles back in. "Let's deal." I fold. Vladimir, yet again, the poker maestro, with a brilliant hand.

Round 7. I have a lousy hand and fold. "What you got Vladimir?" Vlad picks up his cards and lays down a royal flush. Obvious win. Damn it!

"All right guys, last round of the night, anybody need anything? How about you Vlad?" as I shuffle.

Vladimir, with a winner's cockiness says: "Yeah. Since I'm the big winner tonight, why don't you pour me a bourbon. On the rocks." He snickers.

Turn to my roommate: "Can you get it? I'm shuffling."

"Sure man, bourbon. On the rocks. Comin' right up, Vladimir!"

2

Twelve-fifteen AM. Wednesday morning. Nobody in my building is doing laundry right now. It's time to get this done.

I stuff what I find in the hamper into a large cloth bag for the 5 flight journey below.

Doing laundry is the most aggravating activity in the world for me. When I see the machines are already being used by others, I have to wait and drag my cumbersome bag back upstairs. When they aren't being used, it means I have to actually do it and go through the whole process of washing, folding, hanging it, and placing it back into drawers.

It's been so long since I've done laundry last, there are articles in the bag I didn't expect: an old soccer jersey that I had lost, some unknown socks, my cat's favorite toy. Too much separating.

Check the necessary items: detergent, bleach, the money card I need to run the machines. I grab my keys even though I don't lock my apartment door. I drag the bag to the elevator, and hear the ding.

The elevator is small and slow. I step inside with my bag and press "B."

After a few minutes the door opens. It is silent. I hoist my bag over my shoulder and stumble to keep it off the filthy basement floor. I turn a corner and enter the laundry room.

The machines are still. Not churning. I put my bag on the table.

I lift the door of the first machine. It is full of wet clothes. I close the lid. Lift the second, also full of wet clothes. I open the third lid now expecting there to be wet clothes. There are.

I stand there looking at the filled machines. I take a step back and wait several moments wondering.

I step to the first machine, open the lid, scoop out the clothes; panties, bras, towels; all of it, and throw them on the floor. I open the second lid and do the same. And the same with the third. Three heaped piles of wet clothes on the basement floor.

I step back. Have my revenge. After a moment, I throw her clothes in the dryers, one pile at a time.

I fill the washers with my clothes and check my watch and start the machines. I get a real pleasure knowing when to return to the laundry room just as the machines have one final minute left in their cycle. It's a satisfying skill.

Back upstairs in the elevator. Flip on the TV. Nothing of interest on this late at night. I opt to read instead, but keep my eye on the clock.

I hate doing laundry in front of other people. I feel naked. It's my dirty laundry. It's their dirty laundry. Privacy is invaded. That's why I do it late at night. It's my transformation back into a clean world. I don't want anything screwing up that routine.

After 24 minutes my alarm goes off. Perfectly timed. I go out the door knowing I will get there with one minute remaining, just as planned. Ding.

When the elevator door opens in the basement, it is silent. I turn a corner.

My wet clothes are scattered on the filthy floor.

25

D rip. Howl!

My cat crouched in the bathroom door way. Curious, I ran to see the problem, but everything was as usual. Only unusual piece was my cat cringing in the doorway staring up toward the ceiling hissing. I looked up. The ceiling looked normal, no peeling paint, discoloration. After a few minutes, I saw the problem, a drop of water formed on the ceiling, and I watched it fall and splatter on the white tile floor.

My apartment was pleasant enough when I first moved in. It was an old building that required dedicated upkeep, though. The owner wasn't on top of it. Door knobs fell off. Electricity shut off. Toilet wouldn't flush. I renewed the lease anyway, despite that.

The drop finally pushed me over the edge. I still had 10 months left on the lease, and now this. Everyday after that first time, I noticed that water drop would drip only once around 9 P.M. I placed a measuring cup in the spot.

Week 1: 2 ounces.

Week 2: 4 ounces.

Each week it doubled. If so, in six weeks the drop would become a half gallon. Had to call Peter, the super.

9:03 P.M. The drop formed, slowly. Frustration. It fell right in front of our eyes. Peter scoffed: "If that's it and there's no stain, there can't be much water in the ceiling. Don't worry about it."

"Don't worry about it? Are you sure?"

"The ceiling would collapse if there was that much water up there. Call me if it gets worse."

I continued to stare at the ceiling for a while.

The ceiling would collapse…? What could I do to get out of this place?

I grabbed the stepladder, a flashlight, and carefully pressed the palm of my hand against the ceiling. It seemed solid, but water is insidious.

The next night I waited. At 8:50 P.M. I could see the drop slowly forming. Growing, provoking me, mocking me. Splat. "FUCK YOU!"

What if it was poisonous for my cat? Could it flood my apartment and destroy my furniture? Would my cat drown?

Drip.

If the rate of drip continued to accumulate doubling each week, in the final week alone of this lease, 68,719,476,734 ounces of water (9million gallons) would drip through my bathroom ceiling. The accumulation of water flowing over Niagara Falls over 5 days.

I HAD to get out of this lease.

I definitely wouldn't be getting my security deposit back.

26

White room. White table. White chair. Empty glass. Bottle of vodka.

Double shot. Nervous, first drink in six months. Warm stomach.

Relaxed. Looked at the clear glass. Looked at the clear bottle.

My cat leapt onto my lap. I stroked her. She languished. In her own time she got off my lap. The warmth of her body lingered.

I looked at the glass and bottle. The cat's warmth faded. Poured another double. Took it down in one gulp. Feeling faded.

I sat back. Looked at the glass. Looked at the clear bottle.

Again my cat leapt onto my lap. Purred loudly as I stroked her. In her own time, she left.

Looked at the glass. Looked at the bottle.

Reached for the bottle. Aim off. Bottle onto the floor, shattered. I scrambled on to the floor. Hands and knees, desperately trying to salvage what I could as it spread. Licking across the floor I tasted the sting of blood and vodka.

27

I t had been there 2,400 years, far beyond my memory.

Perfect evening, rooftop garden bar, center of Athens. National Geographic view of the Parthenon. Sipped bourbon, eyes transfixed on that awe-inspiring structure. Sun was setting, like a dream. Life was good.

The sound of crickets in the Royal Gardens below drew my attention to its tall, strong pine trees.

...like the pine trees in my backyard. We lived on a corner. My parents wanted to ensure privacy, so they planted young trees, only a few feet tall. They were secured by one poles on either side.

I loved those trees. I practiced soccer, dribbling around them, one tree Roberto Carlos, another Paolo Maldini. We grew together: my first kiss, drink, place I buried my hamster. My brother went off to college. I went to college. They were there for my first job and first girlfriend. Those trees thickened so, I couldn't even walk between them. In time, they became tall, strong pines, like the ones in the Royal Gardens. Eventually my parents sold that home.

I remember driving back years later just to see that old house. Heart sank when I saw the backyard. Stumps. Those magnificent reminders were stolen. The everlasting pines were gone.

"May I get you another?", the bartender interrupted, picking up the empty glass.

"Sure."

The Parthenon was there when Rome fell. The Reformation. The French Revolution, Hiroshima, September 11th.

Those towers were supposed be there forever. They were impressive, dominating the lower part of New York City's skyline. I remember having lunch at Windows on the World, back in 1989 when I was just 7. The view from the 106th floor of the North Tower was spectacular. That all changed into nothing but a mound of warped, molten steel. Flesh and dust. Powerless, I recall feeling defeated watching them collapse live on television. Those everlasting towers were gone.

But the Parthenon still remains. It will always be there.

"Sir? Another?" (silence) "It is amazing, yes?"

"Yes. I've been entranced by the view since the first time I came to this bar."

"Well enjoy it my friend, next month they begin renovations."

"That's OK, at least this view will be here for time to come."

"But you'll never see it from here again. They are closing this bar down for good. Taking down the whole building. You'll have to see it from somewhere else."

I will never see it again, this view of the Parthenon. This rooftop garden. This…

28

T rust me, it's a great place.

Local place. Wine. Bouillabaisse. Time to pay up. Waitress nods. Brings over a small hand written note: 48 euros. Offer my credit card.

"No monsieur, only euros. No credit card."

Shit! No cash left.

"I call a taxi, for you. He will take you for euros, then your hotel."

"Really? You trust the driver to do this?"

She shrugs: "Of course, why would he not?"

"I don't have to come back?"

"No."

48 euro receipt in hand.

Driver is a nice guy, native of Marseille. My curiosity leads to conversation: "Is this kind of thing usual; taxi driver taking the payment?"

"Huh?"

"I mean, this seems odd. I'm giving you the money?"

"Yeah man, of course! That's what we do here in Marseille."

"They trust you to bring it back?"

"I don't bring it back."

Silence.

We pull up to the bank.

"I'll be right back. You gonna wait for me, right?"

"Where else would I go?"

Back in the cab 60 euros in hand. Give him the 48 euros. He accepts it, turns the engine on, and begins to make a U-turn. "Huh? We're going back to the restaurant? Isn't the hotel by the old port?"

"First we give the money to Juliette!"

"So Juliette is the waitress?"

"No, Juliette is Juliette."

He stops a few minutes later, further down the boulevard.

Jumps out. Runs off without a word. Enters a small corner bodega. Three old men sit at a sidewalk table sipping wine. Two minutes later he's back in the cab.

"Everything go OK?"

"Juliette isn't there, but I left the money with Pierre. He will get it to the restaurant, so everything's OK!"

"Hey man, what just happened here? How do you know what Pierre will do?"

"Eh?"

"What happened? Who is Juliette? Who is Pierre?"

He smirks: "To have a restaurant here in Marseille, you must have trust."

"Why didn't you just keep the cash?"

"I don't understand. Why would I cheat Juliette?"

"But you could rake in a fortune. Just take it and run!"

"Why would I do that?"

"You're sitting on a lot of cash! I don't get it! How does Juliette completely trust you?"

"She just does! It's not worth giving up my life, besides, trust is based on threat."

29

A fork in the road.

No fork on my map.

Picked one.

BAM!

Steering wheel jerked left: "SHIT!"

Coasted to the side of the road.

Flat tire.

"Damn it. I'm sure this wouldn't have happened on the other road."

Punched the steering wheel.

Called my girlfriend: "I took the wrong fucking route, got a flat tire. I'm an idiot, and I think I broke my FUCKING finger!"

"Sweetheart, why did you break your finger?"

30

Impossible to avoid that family every day.

Passed them to and from my favorite bar. From the dullness of their eyes and olive skin to the amber beer with its white foamy head.

Went out one evening for a Carlsberg, Rue Saint.-Honoré. Same corner. I approached and saw the child stand up and urinate in the street. Walked by.

Sat at the bar. Finished the beer, went to take a piss in that filthy bathroom. Left.

Their corner. Same misery. The man, woman, child, stank. An ATM right next to them. I withdrew 50 euros and left.

I planned on being in Paris for a single month. This was going to be my month of self-reflection. Went back to that bar to write a bit.

Loved the place. It involved passing their corner every night though.

Day 1. There they sat. Dirty. Their boy pissed in the street.

Beer.

Day 2. They sat. Begged for food.

Beer.

Day 3. They sat. Glass eyed.

Beer.

Day 4.Sat. Shoddy.

Beer.

Day 5. They were not there.

Where were they?

Where the hell were they?

At the bar. Probably some Syrian refugees. Deported? It actually kept me awake.

Day 6. They sat there, again. "Hey, where the hell were you? What, you needed a break?"

He looked up at me: "We got bored with watching you."

32

I wish it were yesterday.

Friday evening, girlfriend came over, dinner and a movie. She ordered and I made ourselves a drink each.

Toy Story. Movie ended. She wanted to get in bed, tired from a long day of work. I wasn't sleepy, but got in bed with her anyway.

I dozed off as she gently snored. Abruptly awoke from a nightmare and checked the clock: 1:17 A.M. Got out of bed. Quietly closed the bedroom door and flicked on the TV. Channel surfed, *Platoon*. Willem Defoe's character was left for dead. The fiery visuals and sounds of gunfire created a cacophony in my head. I absent mindedly refreshed the drink I was having with my girlfriend. Wow! Thousand yard stare.

Stiffness in my throat. Bright lights above me burned into my eyes. A tube in my nose. Instinctively jerked my hands to remove another tube I felt in my throat. I was restrained. Couldn't speak. Parents, brother and girlfriend stood at the foot of my bed crying. My hands were shaking and tears rolled down my cheeks.

Someone entered the room and removed the tube. Pain. Still couldn't speak. Where was I? What happened? Trembling, I struggled to motion to my family for paper and pen:

What is happening?
Where am I?
Can you call therapist?
Is cat ok?

"The level of alcohol in your body was so high you experienced respiratory failure – near lethal." I shuddered, turned my face away. More tears.

I.V.s. Vitals on a screen to my left. Day passed, staring at the ceiling, my family sitting by anxiously. The monotonous beeping kept me aware of being in the ICU. Nurses and doctors filed through. I was shaking, anxious, and ashamed.

Although vitals returned to normal, it wasn't enough to relieve my anxiety and shame. When evening arrived my family left. I felt powerless.

Night was difficult. Every hour I was awakened by staff to check if I was still conscious. It felt like a nightmare, but I knew it was real. Fear and shame.

I wish it were yesterday.

22

You spics! Always the same! Trying to rip me off! Wearing some stupid 'Proud to be American' T-shirt. Get out!

"Nah man, I'm telling you, I gave you a twenty, you gotta give me the right change."

Guy behind me gives me a nudge, yells: "Yeah man, fuck this stupid deli guy. Fuckin towelhead." He gives a wink and I notice him slip a few packs of gum and a lollipop into his pocket.

I turn back to the cashier: "Fine, whatever. I'm not coming here anymore. Keep your stupid ten bucks."

The door jingles as I step back outside onto 30th Avenue right by Crescent Street.

A moment later the guy who was behind me jingles the door. Laughing: gum, lollipop displayed to me. "This is a how a real American does it!"

I didn't even have a chance to respond before the cashier barged out.

"Hey you damn spic! You stole from me! Oh I see, you two are in it together!" as he pointed at both of us.

Thief shouted back: "Fuck you buddy! I don't even know this fucking spic!"

"I'm calling the cops now! You both were in it!"

"Go ahead call the cops. I will fuck you up man." He thumped his chest.

I stepped in. "Guys, calm down."

The thief glared at me: "Fuck off spic."

I responded: "Leave the guy alone."

"Fuck off."

Cashier raised his fist at us: "I'll call the cops on you both!"

The thief leapt forward lashing out his fist as I stepped between them, catching it.

Blood dripped on my shirt as he bolted toward Newtown Avenue.

I pressed on my swollen lip to control the bleeding, and turned toward the cashier.

He gave me the evil eye: "You got what you deserved," as he slammed the door behind him, with a jingle.

31

Two-fifteen A.M. Downtown train arrives. Doors open. Friend and I enter.

Homeless guy stretched out on a seat. "Got any change?"

"Sorry buddy." We pass into the next car. Another homeless guy.

"Got any change?"

"Sorry buddy." We pass into the next car. Another homeless guy.

"Got any change?"

Friend hands the guy a dollar. We finally sat down.

"Why did you give that guy a dollar?"

Lightning Source UK Ltd.
Milton Keynes UK
UKHW041405280119
336340UK00001B/83/P